Butterfish and gheefish and other nonsense stories

Butterfish and gheefish and other nonsense stories

Swetha Prakash

With a Foreward by *SHANTHERI MALLAYA*

Butterfish and gheefish and other nonsense stories

First Edition by Zero Degree Publishing: January 2022

ISBN: 978-81-949739-1-1
ZDP Title: 2

ZERO DEGREE PUBLISHING
No.55(7), R Block, 6th Avenue,
Anna Nagar,
Chennai - 600 040

Website: www.zerodegreepublishing.com-
E Mail id: zerodegreepublishing@gmail.com
Phone : 89250 61999

Typeset: Vidhya Velayudham
Printed in India

Author's Preface

Nonsense literature is as old as human history itself though it was made spectacularly popular by Lewis Carroll's Alice books and the poems of Edward Lear. Samples of nonsense literature can be found in all cultures and all civilisations. This book takes the nonsense genre further and focuses on nonsense flashfiction. Nonsense literature believes in joyous writing, it does not believe in classical structures and it deals with ideas and the playful presentation of ideas.

To write a collection of nonsense stories you as a writer need a nurturing space where you can experiment on literary forms and write those stories that are talking to you in your dreams. Dr Lakshmi Priya and her literary consultancy Pachyderm Tales have provided just the same and thus made this book possible. I cannot thank her and Pachyderm tales enough.

Swetha Prakash

October 2021

FOREWORD

I recall my mother, a prolific reader herself, ruing recently, saying, “Laughter and humour have become distinct afterthoughts in this age. Young people rarely enjoy a joke wholeheartedly. They think it’s uncool to laugh at something they perceive as silly or nonsense. Everything has to be smart to appear funny.” I couldn’t but help agreeing with her sharp observation. Too much intellectualization is a problem in this day and age. People bend backwards, sweat to write or say something intelligent and funny. Is fun so much of an effort?

That is where I must say I find nonsense literature very refreshing. As a term it could very well inspire different reactions in the mind of the listener or the reader – that of incredulity, a smirk, a smile, anything. I would put it as one of the world’s oldest, most consumed yet most underrated genres of literature.

Swetha Prakash's "Butterfish and gheefish and other nonsense stories" is nonsense in all its purity, simply because it takes the young and the not-so-reader to a world of sheer joy - animals, birds, insects, reptiles, princesses all interlocked in "nonsense". The author has used a mix of imagery and text to create myriad reams of suspension of belief effortlessly bringing together elements of nature in simple narrative.

The author is a friend, an accomplished writer, Indophile who constantly thirsts for new areas to explore. Her dynamism and zeal for academic study, for presentation and for writing leaves me amazed, so much so that I have in jest labelled her as "possessing an abnormal appetite for achievement".

Having followed her works and having read her earlier books such as "Padma Goes to Space" and her other book in the nonsense genre," "How the eland twisted its horns", it comes as no surprise to me that she leaves a trail of profound thought even in nonsense. And with "butterfish, gheefish", she takes the nonsense to the next level with flash fiction.

Besides the title story – The story of the moving suitcase, The story of the flesh eating grass, How fireflies became immune to fire, The story of the fish tank rank among my favourites – I was grinning at "I guess wild grasses are quite wild..so I guess they can do almost anything" in "The story of the flesh eating grass", while I was marvelling at way Swetha has used titles. Nonsense clearly is irreverent to all conventions of how you would want to structure a story. Each of the 30 pieces leaves you either smiling or tutting away saying "this is downright silly" – and that is precisely the objective of this collection – celebrating being unpretentiously silly.

I envisage a world where nonsense literature reclaims its cultural roots and traditions as an integral part of everyday life – as a part of dinner and lunch conversations in families, at the workplace, among communities, in art and theatre. Nonsense literature can provide interesting wordplay for children and open up a great space for their imagination. The grown up world can indulge in nonsense to relieve itself of the stress of everyday life. "The story of the butterfish and ghee fish and other stories" opens up this world to spontaneous reading and conversation. After all, sense actually begins with nonsense.

SHANTHERI MALLAYA

Shantheri Mallaya has been a journalist for 16 years. Besides, she's a theatreperson, author of a novella, a podcaster and a social cause volunteer.

Contents

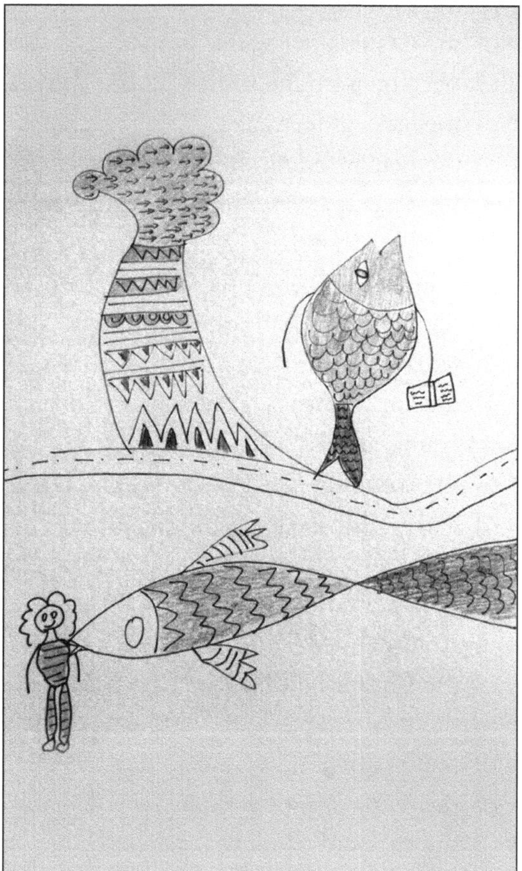

The story of Butterfish and Gheefish

Once upon a time, there was a butterfish. She was a crimson and pink coloured butterfish. She loved eating butter (Amul type yaar) and brinjal (bharta types). She was rather fensible to look at – with butter smeared all over. She was rather fensibly sensible too (or as sensible as you can be in a nonsense story). And due to this sensibility she did a few strange things:

1. She brayed by the Bulberry Tree
2. She quailed a notebook full of letters
3. She was asking questions about a neighbouring red bug

She was a swell butterfish to know on the whole. She was called (and yes she had a name) butterfins. Now there was butterfins and there was gheefins. Gheefins was covered all over with ghee and had the habit of doling out cotton-fish dolls to friendly passerby. Thus, she was also known as dollfins. On festival days, she would give out affection to those who where love surplused. She was a generally useless kind of gheefish. Both the fishes swam together once and that was the end of their story, as they drowned in glee.

Fishtime Watersong

Once there were two fowls – Peafowl and Henfowl. Across the bridge, as they escaped the fourflies, they paused. It was a dance of life – for the four flies were from storyteller kingdom. In this kingdom there was a fish called Fish. It swam three crore miles away from the tyranny of the graded book. It was fishing for information at a local shrine.

Inside the shrine were the inner chambers of Goddess who could make you giddy with her quaint ways. Information found, the fish returned to storyteller kingdom. He was feeling rather faint and thought of a water song – Water here, water there, waterstops by the waterdrop.

By the rainstorm there was a little waterdrop drunk by the fish as he hopped.

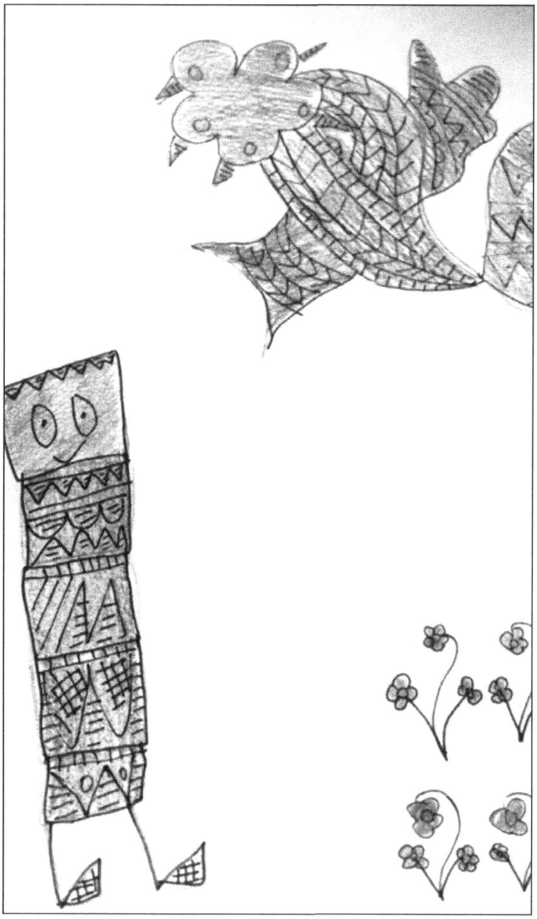

The story of the moving suitcase

Once upon a time, there was a moving staircase. It was moving in from afar. It sung a song as it boarded a spiced jet.

To home, as the springboards swing

To home and much jest.

"So, where was home"?

"Home is where the art is," the moving suitcase answered rather effusively. It was a moving suitcase after all and most probably moved around too often.

In a new minute, the doors opened. It was a strange minute. The five headed bird was there.

"Where?" a curious listener asked.

The doors opened in Two Two Land.

22 land was a strange place with wild flowers and sun flowers. The sunflowers lit up the rainforests, while the wild flowers were being harvested in the fields. The wild flowers were blood red and tasted like honey. A certain playfulness descended upon the five headed bird. He eagerly welcomed the moving suitcase.

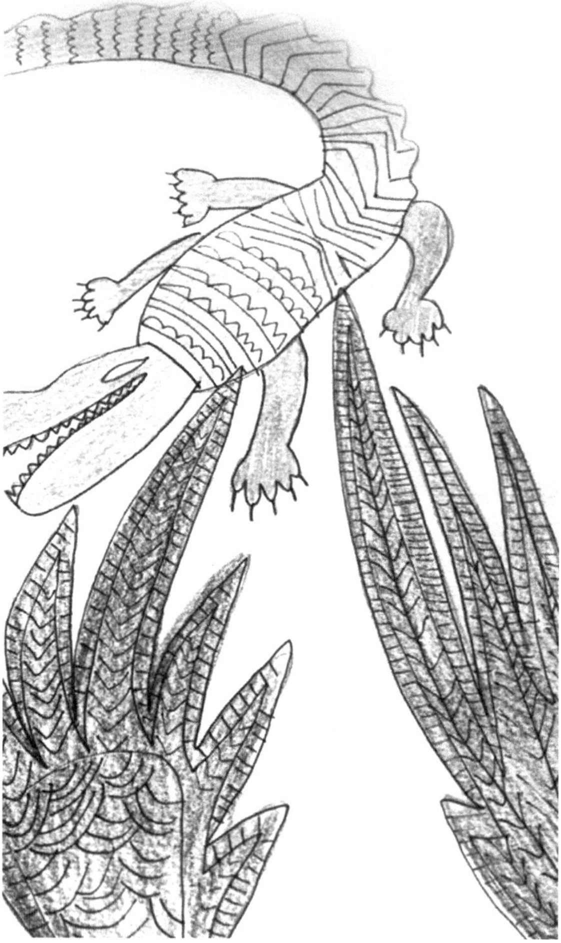

The story of the flesh eating grass

There was once a wildgrass, that grew on the cliffs of San Placibo, that developed a taste for crocodile flesh. It learnt to crawl all the way up to the cliff everyday and hide in a cave mouth till a crocodile will pass by. And then, he would leap on the crocodile. He would unflesh the crocodile and dine happily on the skin. He would feel happy only after he gobbled a few hundred crocodiles.

"Hundred crocodiles. How many where there?"

"Zazillions, it was the land of the crocodiles. San Placibo was croc land and no other predators lived there till the wildgrass appeared on the scene.

The crocodiles were initially shocked by what was happening. But soon they realised something was eating them up from inside – how could a wild grass consume crocodile flesh?

"I guess wild grasses are quiet wild.. so I guess they can do almost anything," one crocodile said.

"That makes sense," another crocodile said.

"Sure," said another crocodile, whose neighbour had just be eaten, rather briskly.

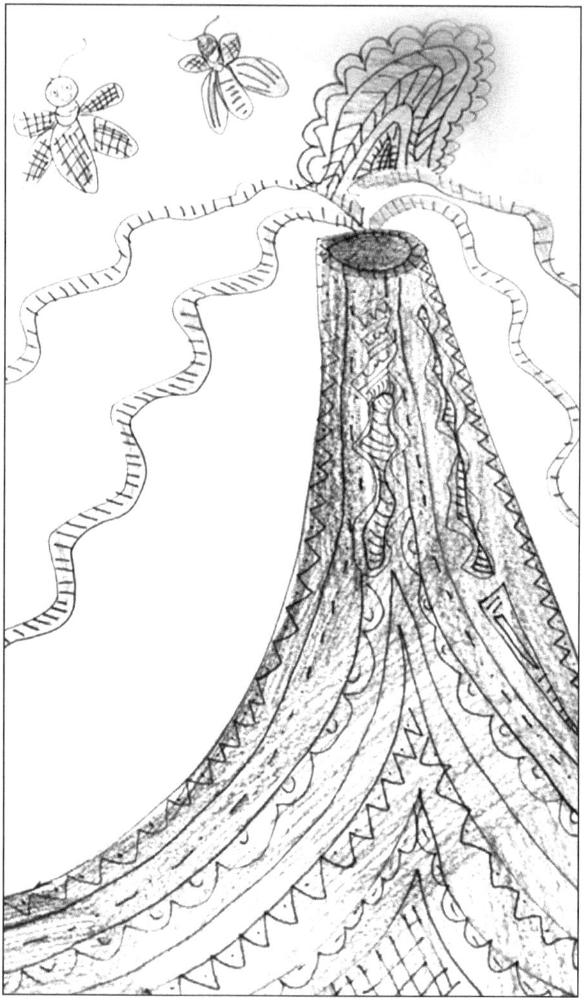

How fireflies became immune to fire..

There was once a firefly Miffly that was immune to fire flames. It was flitting across the river and found an erupting volcano. Another firefly, Crass flew past it. This firefly was not immune to fire and soon erupted into flames. There was a point to be made is wrong. There was not.

"For we are together," sang the dying firefly.

At once the Firefly Miffly felt bad about being immune to the flames.

"I am joining you," cried Miffly and flew into the lava and emerged only after a second.

"For we are together," sang the dying firefly.

"Rub the flames on your shoulders, and dance. You will be safe."

And so safe was the other Firefly Crass. And after that day, all fireflies were immune to the fire.

The story of the lisping deer

Here and now,

"I am a snailrock," Birdy introduces herself.

Birdy is crazy about rocks and walks.

She is not a snailrock. She just likes saying she is a snailrock. The reason she is saying she is a snailrock is because she is constantly flowering inside with pleasant calmness. It was a sort of unbroken dream – o being a feather light snailrock.

"But what is a snail rock Birdy?"

"Any snail-shaped rock.."

"What do snail rocks do Birdy? Surely, they sing to lisping deers?"

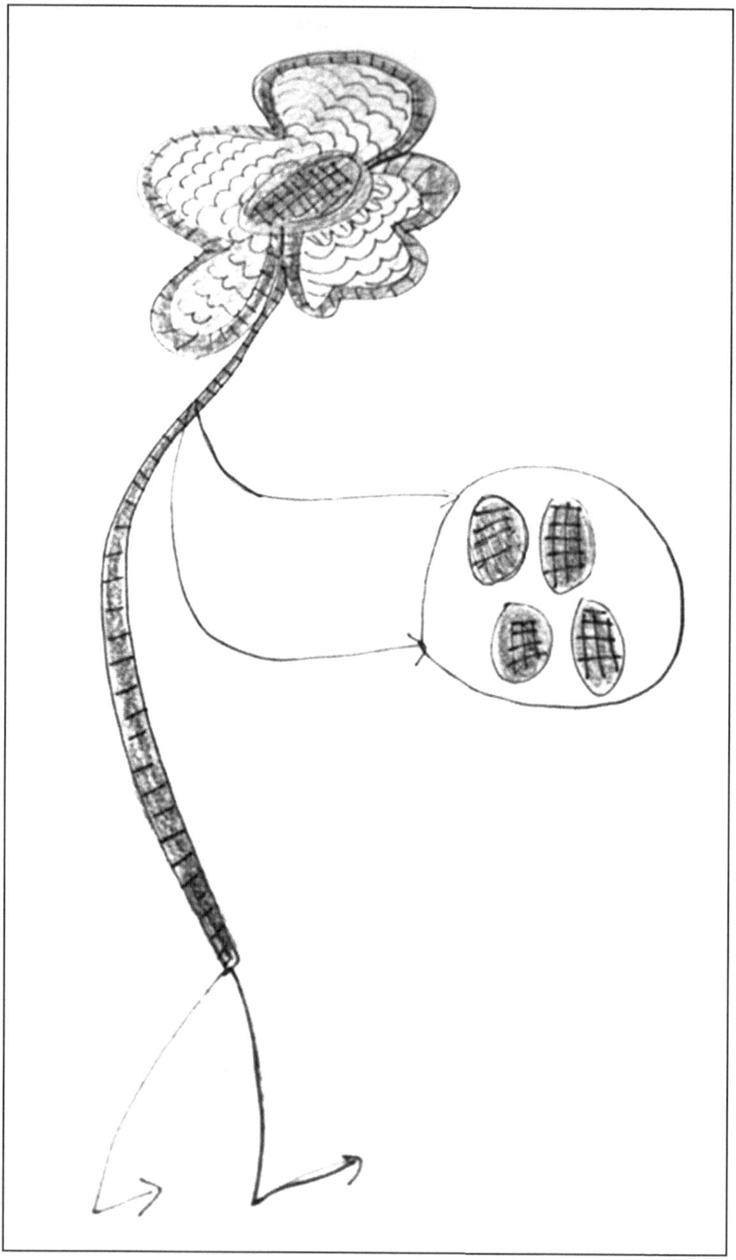

The story of the nectar hiding flower

Once upon a time there was a nectar hiding flower. It had the sweetest nectar in all the worlds and it went and hid the nectar somewhere. No one was able to find the elixir.

One day this flower found some sweet bird eggs. They were eagle eggs. These also looked like they were very good to consume. So, it went and hid them in a gasket.

This nectar hiding flower then went to sleep, and slept and slept and slept and slept and slept. One day it woke up and went to drink its nectar. But it could not find it. It found the eagle's eggs but it was vegetarian. Hungry and tired, it went back to sleep.

The No Yes Bird

How was there a no/yes bird? There was a no/yes bird because there was, because there was.

How was there a no/yes bird? There was a no/yes bird because it was smart, it was.

How was there a no/yes bird? There was a no/yes bird because it knew how to write and sing songs.

How was there a no/yes bird? There was a no/yes bird because the impossibility is only what you think is impossible.

The hay pile and the straw

Once upon a time, there was a story. It got lost but Avistra found it. It was a story about a hay pile and a straw. The straw was dozing in the sun and rivers of sweat were forming along its forehead and falling on the haypile it was resting on. It was getting hotter and hotter. And the haypile was getting wetter and wetter. The sun was feeling thirsty. Suddenly she saw that the hay pile had a lot of water. She bent down and drank the water. The straw slept while the hay pile laughed.

The nonsense tale of the fresh water fish and the housefly

Once upon a there, there lived a freshwater fish. She was smart and supple, and was called Do-little-dupple. Do-little-dupple could sing and fly and was often seen playing with the housefly. The housefly called Quite-full-and-thank-you, was filled with black blank spaces and full stops.

"You are quite a sentence in yourself," said the freshwater fish Do-little-dupple.

"Í will try to live through that sentence," said Quite-full-and-thank-you, the housefly.

"You make all miniature toys tense," said Do-little-dupple.

"That is a sad fact," said Quite-full-and-thank-you.

As it was.

The story of the fishing net and the claypot

There was once a storyteller. She was called Florine Furnace. This is a story of story she once narrated in Scandinavia. This story was about a fishing net and clay pot. This story was thought up by Myka, a little girl in South India. She had dreamt of this story and had a very colourful dream at that. She dreamt that both the fishing net and the clay pot used to give her gifts – gifts of fish and gifts of fruits. The root of the problem for her was to find a Keeper of Gifts who could keep all the gifts for her.

Now why did she want a keeper of gifts? Being young she had read a lot of old fashioned princess stories where the princesses always had Keepers of something or the other. Naturally she wanted to be like the heroine of these stories from very very long ago.

"Why is my hand talking to me?" she asked one day of the clay pot.

"Your Highness," and that is how the claypot addressed her, "what a thing to have done. The whole world will come undone.

There was a fast charged horse – he was nutty, as he was hoarse.

He was nutty, as he was horse. His hand too started speaking to him - and boy did the world come undone."

"You are scaring me oh claypot," said Myka

"Ohhhh, I am?" responded the Claypot

"Yes, and the hand is talking again," said a scared Myka

"What is it saying? Which hand is it?" asked the Claypot.

"It is the left hand. What is it saying? It is saying 'Kill the false news.' Yes, that is what it is saying – 'Kill the false news.'

"What your hand seems to be into media studies?" asked the Fishing Net

"It is, is it not?" said the little girl Myka

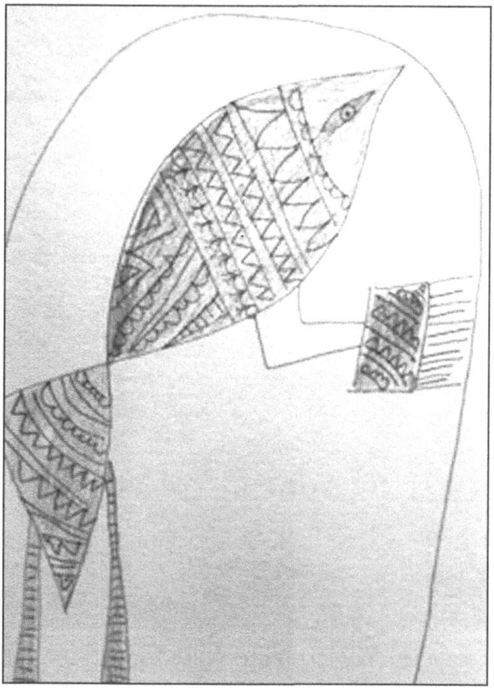

The story of writing on the wall

There was a fish called Writing on the Wall. It was soothing through the duststorms. What was it soothing? It was soothing a Soothsayer's lair. The lair was dusty and unkempt. Callabus was tired of living in the Indian Ocean and had relocated to the Soothsayer's lair. The soothsayer's lair was beside the River Sadhana. Tiny spiralling greenflowers grew aplenty along the river Banks. Three folds of a white sari covered the Soothsayer's lair. There was a frog called Wrapping Teeth that lived by the River Sadhana.

At the heart of the forest by the river brook there was an abandoned witches' den. This is where lived Wrapping Teeth.

"It is time you learnt your own name," Wrapping Teeth told Writing on the Wall.

"I know my name pretty well," said Writing on the Wall

"Do you? That is a good thing then," said Wrapping Teeth

The story of the Crafty Bear

Once upon a time, there was a very very thirsty bear. His name was Space Changer. He lived in a place called Wristside town. Along the fabulous days, he was trailing along a way. He sung a song and ate a mysore masala dosa. The dosa was lined with spicy chilly chutney and mashed up potatoes. It was crispy and hot. And crumbled in his hands.

Suddenly he heard a voice.

"I am your teacher,"

Space Changer looked up and saw the noon sun. It had almost set.

Space Changer loved it when the sun changed colours and sparkled brightly in the blood coloured sky.

He was bleeding. He was bleeding because whenever he didn't get water his gums would bleed. Which was a good thing because he was a Vampyre bear. Because he was of a non violent nature he would only drink his own blood.

The quiet was quite deadly

All along the Dead Sea, there lived a Dead Fish and a bee. They were the only creatures you could see. All along there were summer fares. The liar of the Dead fish and bee was an old cave lined with dead leaves. There was a deadly silence. 12% is left. 12% of the silence is left. The rest just evaporated with the contagion plan. It would have been good if we could wipe down the windscreens. We were wiping out an entire civilised practice. Not an entire civilisation.

Stories are opposing logical death at all times.

"Yes, and I remember, there is no dialogue in this story. What use is a nonsense story without dialogue?"

The story of the climbing fish

Death as a certainty and an impossibility. There was a climbing fish and it was climbing a water fall. It kept climbing and falling. Falling and climbing. It was climbing and falling. Falling and climbing.

As it climbed and climbed it found that beyond a point it was not falling.

Then feeling rather Mad she jumped to the next waterfall and feel directly into the jaws of a ghariyal. All this happened in the Ganges.

The story of Slaying Dragon

Once upon a time there was a flying dinosaur called Slaying Dragon. She was a rather intriguing flying dinosaur. She loved chasing feathered dragons. She lost half her brain when a dragon claw entered her head. She bled out some brain stuff but was otherwise quiet finished. Or so everyone thought. But as it happened -

"What do you want?" someone asked her.

"I am here to answer your questions, if you can answer mine," she said.

"We can't answer your questions Slaying Dragon, our brains may be clawed out too," said a youthful Dinosaur. He was a T-Rex not a Pteranodon and hence was hoping to make a meal of Slaying Dragon once she flew back to the ground.

Wince upon a time…

Wince upon a tyme, there was a King. He always wore a crown on his head so guess he must have been a King. He owned four kingdoms or so the documents said. In the first kingdom there was a drought. In the second there was a flood. In the third there was a cyclone. And in the fourth he lived.

The deepening desire for the King was to adopt a cat. He had a strange love for cats and they kept appearing in his dreams. Of all the cats Vasili was the best. This could have been Vasili's story but it was not. It was neither the King's story. It was the King's river's story. Now this river was a smart river. It knew it could remove the drought, stop the flood and divert the cyclone.

Now the 'I' died in the King.

The 'I' died and turned into 'We'

Now the river was at 'I' only. It never lost its "I"

Moral of the story: Rivers have 'I' in them.

Padmavathi and the Snarling Serpent

Once upon the Tyne, Padmavathi was perceiving clearly. It was the best of tides. It was the worst of tides. She was at a seashore. There was some good seabreeze. It was @ affection that she decided that drowning in mirth was useless. It was glassnot day. Why was she blushing? Because she had eaten a pink rose. Put its drying petals in her mouth. She wanted to taste a bud now. A white jasmine bud.

"I will write in African, you in English," said she to the Snarling Serpent.

"I thought you were Indian," the Snarling Serpent, who was very much a cobra replied.

"I am," said Padmavathi

"So am I sad," said the Snarling Serpent, fishing for more information.

The Girl who transcended Time

Once upon a teeming stirring story. There was a glum universe. And in the center of this universe there was a glummer Plum. Plum was not plant based nutrition. He was a real human being.

He liked the folk tradition. He knew of the world were women changed to trees and were cut down for their good wood. And thus the glumness. There was girl who changed into an infinity. This was supposed to be her story.

"How can a girl change into infinity?"

"Through quantum mechanics you fool, there is no other way,"

"Break the time-space continuum,"

"What was this gurl's name, she who transcended time?"

"That is her name – she who transcended time."

"What rubbish.."

"No really, the rumour went that she had thrown out her old name and was to be called with the first name that was created for her. And you were the one who made up the first name."

"So where can I find the Girl who transcended time?"

"On Earth, you can find her on Earth."

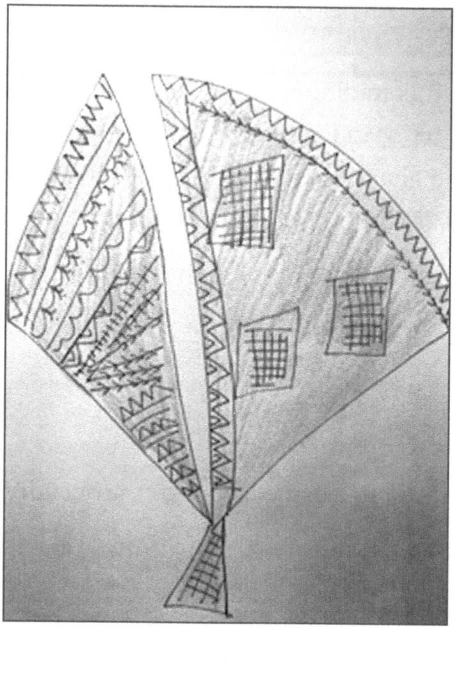

The story of the vanquished Heat

Once upon a weather, the vanquished heat was thinking of reviving itself with a fan. She liked fancy things like the fan. They went swish swosh. And swosh swish. Well, you know how fancy things go. This what she really liked the swish swoshing fan and the swosh swishing fan. It was a pink swish swoshing fan.. Mild peach colored actually. It even tasted like peach. It had three diamonds placed on it.. The diamonds, she could almost breathe them. She loved touching their shiny furs.

"Furs on diamonds?"

"In our country diamonds grow furs"

"Can you wear the furs?"

"On your hands yes."

The story of the fish tank

Once upon a time, three fishes who knew everything lived very happily in a fish tank. There were five tiger cubs that lived along the shore. These were busy writing cute nonsense stories. The tiger cubs were busy composing when they were interrupted by a wholesome meal provided by a neighbour. They were saying only one thing –

"Let the fishtanks fill."

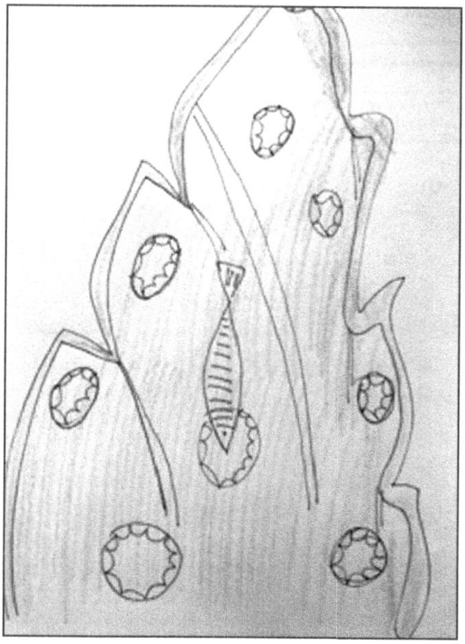

The story of the quailfish

Once upon a time, there was a quailfish. It was nice and friendly. It lived by the Yellow bay. It was the founder of a new order. It had a fondness for merry go rounds. It loved yellow merry go arounds and there were many of those around yellow bay. It longed for some yellow mushrooms which grew on graves. And it longed for lemon curds – yellow and yellow some more. It was bushwalking along the bushes when it was swallowed by a giant quailfish eating brown anthill. The brown anthill lived happily ever after. It even turned yellow.

The story of the living woodcase

There are three ways to the bridge to Placelands. There are three wayfinders in the path to wisdom. The critical thinking needed to precipice the discussion is missing. That the land of nonsense is not making any sense and that the sensibility of falsehood has taken over. That the waterstoves are not working and that the woodcase has come to life. The story has ended but we had hoped to find the beginning.

The story of the storylad

There was a strange bison that lived along long side park. There were three ways of seeing and several of being. The belonginess that went with the cloistered airspace never left her. There were strange wild yearnings left by the doorknob. There was a storylad. He lived by the Bullet Train stop. His name was Wild Whiskers. He was straying for a coffee by the Nilgris when estrangement took over - the three thrills of disillusionment with the Marxists took over and he sipped his coffee sweetly. There was a nigh tower of differences. The splitscreen moment of wandering left us joyous.

The old tunnelway Paradise Won

There was a quaint old tunnelway that leads to Pathway Bliss. It was known as Paradise Won. It was close to ramshackle huts, that flamed up during the summer. It was made of solid gold and liquid silver. It was paranoid that there was another like it in the world. So, it sent out a message to all the tunnelways, proposing a strength competition.

It was the nature of being to cast away sideways, to find the strange correlations between equations unfed and underfed.

It was a place of wiseness, a true Kadambari. In was at this intersection that the 'I-ness' was lost. It was at this transaction, that points connected and disconnected. He won the competition.

Cat and cat

When the sentence falls it should be music to the brain. Carnatic Music. The ceremony of cremation grounds is strange and fabulous to the ears. It is a crowdsouring way of being. We are at the best edge. A small cat crossed the door, it was fleeing an even smaller cat. Soon tombstones opened up and we found the writing on the wall. The cat was whispering to itself and making very little sound. It was hoping to find some fried fish that it could eat for the day. It was called Augusta. There was little time for studies. It was all so well meaning and sensible that the ontology of rabbits fleeing from their predators could not be understood. It was a rapid speed-reading technique that caught everyone's attention. It was a second to non storybook with a beginning, middle and end. It was through this book that the taxonomy of speech could be read. The cat and its cat pursuer and chasing windmills ran across the gate where a hailstorm is resting.

The hailstorm is well formed and sneezing away. The cats could feel the sneeze of the hailstorm and tried to run away. It was a fine run across the center of the earth where there where a lot of magnets. The magnets were manmade and alienmade. The earth and sky magnets looked at each other with wonder. They smiled and gazed at the magnetless moon. No businessman showed any interest in the book.

The levitating act

The class act that was the doledrum strung at us as something strange, we attained and we attained at enlightenment. Light strewed from across the room and flooded the flooring. There were three fences and four cattleranges. The cattle could not hop over the fences. The doorways and the highways were neigh the way – neighed the horses. The fried gateway to being and non being, was the title of the book that lay in the refrigerator. The economics of being lazy made sense to the car finally. The frail kitten and sense boys made no sense of the worlds within. It was a scary day being scared was something like being scared. The similar ring found on the baker and the prince left the kingdom in disray. The hat and the hatter were both found levitating.

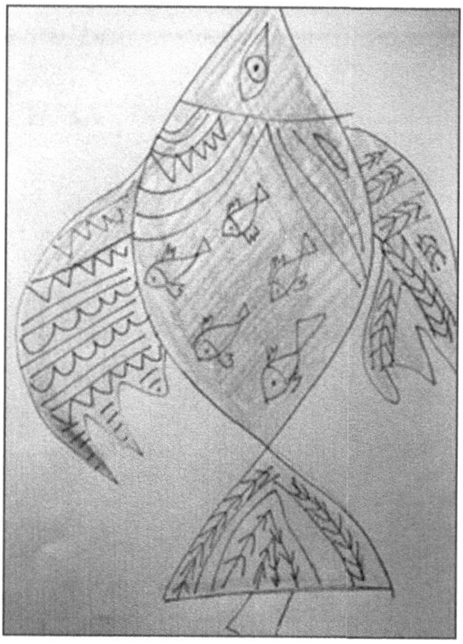

The story of the fish

The nature of emptiness like a fish fluttering in a fishing net, tense and torn. The nature of being like a flown fish that finds flying tedious. The images of a sameside basket where lay strewn the remains of dead fishes and their boons. I am the God of Flying fishes. I know it is unfashionable these days to be the God of anything. But still they sometimes allow us – the Gods of Flying Fishes. They do so to ensure a steady population of flying fishes to their markets.

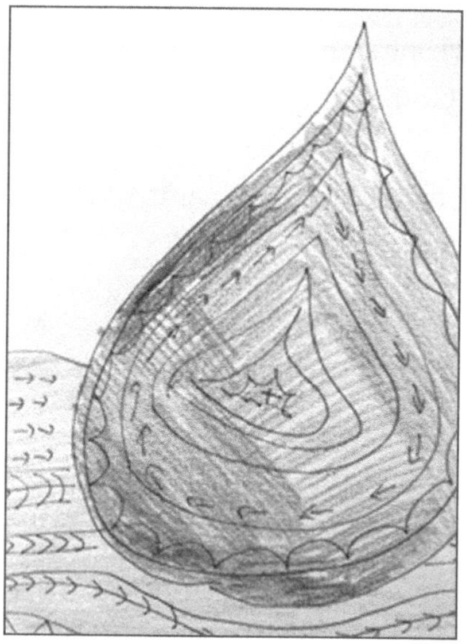

The story of floating fig

The Floating Fig was once asked by his disciples if he believed in form or emptiness.

"Neither form nor emptiness," was his reply.

What else then?" they persisted

"I believe in nothingness"

"So, emptiness you mean?"

"No not in emptiness, Nothingness,"

"How is emptiness different from nothingness?"

"When you empty emptiness of its form you get nothingness."

About the Author

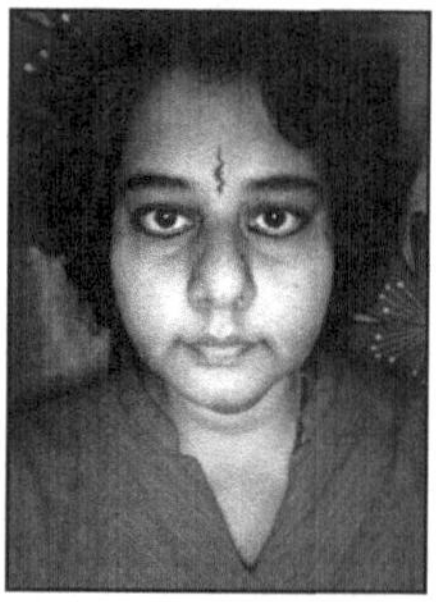

Swetha Prakash's nonsense book – "The Monster Book of limericks" has been previously been published by Unison, Bangalore. Swetha has been a recipient of the Charles Wallace India Trust award by the British council to study post modernism and creative writing at the Scottish Union's International Summer school, University of Edinburgh. She has also been a recipient of the Scottish Book Trust and Times Jura New Writer Award where she was awarded a month's writer's residency at the uninhabited Hebridian Isle of Jura. Swetha has completed her MA in Writing at the University of Warwick. Swetha's book "Padma Goes to Space" is a bestseller and was highly ranked in the media as one of the best children's books to come out of India. She has narrated stories at the Bangalore Literature Festival, Bookaroo, Katha Utsav, National Conference on Sanskrit for children, iGennext Leadership Forum and the Varanasi Children's Literature Festival. Swetha's latest two children's books are "How the eland twisted its horns" and "Pi Chart" both published by Ukiyoto. Swetha is the author of the nonfiction book "Indian Storytelling Traditions" and the collection of poems "Climate Talk."